First published in Great Britain in 2019 by Pat-a-Cake
This edition published in 2019

ISBN: 978 1 52638 276 4 • 10 9 8 7 6 5 4 3 2 1
Pat-a-Cake, an imprint of Hachette Children's Group,
Part of Hodder & Stoughton Limited
Carmelite House, 50 Victoria Embankment, London EC4Y 0DZ
An Hachette UK Company
www.hachette.co.uk • www.hachettechildrens.co.uk
Printed in China

My Very First Story Time

Snow White and the Seven Dwarfs

Retold by Ronne Randall
Illustrated by Sophie Rohrbach

Snow White

The Seven Dwarfs

mirror

The Queen

castle
cottage
apple
Prince
horse

Snow White was a beautiful princess who lived in a castle with her wicked stepmother, the Queen.

Every day, the Queen looked into her magic mirror and said, "Mirror, mirror, on the wall, who's the fairest one of all?"

"You are," the mirror answered.

But one day, the mirror said something different.

"Snow White is the fairest!"

The Queen was so angry! She told her huntsman to take Snow White deep into the forest and leave her there.

"I am so sorry," the huntsman told Snow White, leading her away.

Poor Snow White! The forest felt full of danger.

As darkness fell, she came to a cosy little cottage. The door was open, so in she went.

Inside she found seven dwarfs eating dinner.

“Who are you?” they asked.

When Snow White told them about her wicked stepmother, they said she could stay with them.

At the castle, the Queen went back to her mirror.

"Mirror, mirror, on the wall, who's the fairest one of all?" she asked.

The mirror replied, "In a cottage, in the forest lives kind Snow White, she is the fairest!"

The Queen flew into a fury. "I must find her!" she screamed.

Next morning, as the dwarfs left for work, they told Snow White to stay indoors. "That way you will be safe from the Queen," they said.

Snow White was reading when there was a knock at the door. There stood an old woman with a basket of rosy red apples.

“Will you buy some of my juicy red apples?” the old woman asked. “They’re delicious. Try one and see!”

As soon as Snow White bit into the apple, she fell down in a faint. The old woman – who was really the wicked Queen in disguise – had poisoned it!

The wicked Queen ran off laughing. "Now she'll never come back," she cackled. "And I will once again be the fairest one of all!"

As the wicked Queen disappeared into the forest, the seven dwarfs came home. They were so upset to find Snow White lying there, pale and still.

As the dwarfs were trying to wake Snow White, a handsome young prince came riding by. The moment he saw Snow White, he fell in love with her.

"Perhaps I can wake her," he told the dwarfs. "Please let me try."

The prince knelt down and gently lifted Snow White's head. The piece of poisoned apple fell from her lips. Suddenly her eyes opened wide – she was awake!

Snow White looked into the prince's eyes and her heart filled with love.

As the prince took Snow White in his arms, the dwarfs smiled joyfully. They could see that the prince and Snow White were really in love – and would live happily ever after.

Count the chairs! Which table has the right number of chairs for the seven dwarfs?

Can you spot five differences between these two pictures?